MW00942676

Christmas with Bernadette

Book Two in the Bernadette Series

EMILY GRACE ORTEGA

illustrated by
Meg Ross Whalen

Copyright © 2014 by Emily Grace Ortega.
Published by Santa Fe Catholic Books.
ISBN-13: 978-1500966966
ISBN-10: 1500966967

First written edition 2014.

https://www.createspace.com/4970137

for Felicity, my Christmas baby
-E.G.O.

for Danny
-M.R.W.

Contents

It's Beginning to Look a Lot like Advent

CHAPTER ONE

I hopped into the minivan after school. It had been a great day in first grade at St. Cletus, and Mama's navy blue car was already there, waiting for me. That made it a really great day. "Mama!" I exclaimed as I climbed up into the car, "Advent! Did you know that Advent is starting up on Sunday? That means we're coming right up toward Christmas!"

"Christmas?" Victor asked from the backseat where he was buckled. "For real, Bernadette? Christmas?" Victor is my brother. He's four. He barely remembers last time we had Christmas. A few times in the summer we snuck into the storage closet together and got out our Christmas stockings. We just wanted to look at them. They're so beautiful. Mine is dark, dark red with sparkly snowflakes. It has a thick white stripe across the top where Great-Grandma Anne embroidered *Bernadette* in perfectly beautiful letters. Victor's is dark, dark green with St. Nicholas and a huge sack of toys. His name goes across the top of his, too. One time, though, Mama caught us and said we're not allowed to do that. Great-Grandma put a lot of hard work and love into those stockings, and she was not about to have them left on the floor and eaten by the dog. I wouldn't have left them on floor for the dog. But we didn't do it again after that.

"For real, Victor!" I answered. "Right, Mama?"

"Right you are, Bernadette. But Advent lasts a long time. It's best not to be too excited about Christmas yet. We need to focus on Advent while it's here. What did Miss D say about Advent?"

"Oh, not too much," I said. Miss D is my teacher. Mama knows that she always talks about important things like Advent. "She just talked about candles and stuff. Then we worked on learning an Advent song. 'Come On, Come On, You Mean Well,' it's called."

Mama bunched up her mouth in a puzzled way and turned to look at me from her spot behind the steering wheel. My other brother, Matthew, who isn't even two yet, screamed and threw his stuffed ducky at me. Even Victor is mature enough not to do that.

"NO, Matthew! Don't throw in the car," Mama said. She turned back to me, "Bernadette, don't give Spotted Ducky back to Matthew. He'll just throw it again. 'Come On, Come On, You Mean Well'?" She was definitely puzzled.

"Yes," I replied. "You know it. We're always singing it at church before Christmas. I just never knew the words before. Like this," I started singing, "come on, come on, you mea-ea-ean well…"

"Oh! You mean 'O Come, O Come, Emmanuel!'"

"Well, I guess it does start with 'O.' You're right about that." Sometimes it's hard to tell why grown-ups don't understand what I'm talking about.

*   *   *

Before dinner on Sunday, Daddy explained a little more about Advent. Mama lit a single candle on a wreath while he was talking. She left three candles standing there, unlit and cold.

"Mama! Light the rest of the candles!" Victor waved his arms in the air.

"Victor, you know how to ask nicely," Mama corrected.

"Mama, would you PLEASE light the rest of the candles?" Victor said.

Mama smiled. "No," she said. "Each Sunday before Christmas, we'll light one more candle. So next week, we'll have two candles burning. When all four candles are lit, then it's almost Christmas!"

I smiled at the thought of it being "almost Christmas!"

Victor was just worried about the candles. "Then I get to blow it out!" he cried.

"Victor, you know how to—"

"Mama, may I PLEASE blow it out?" he interrupted Mama to ask nicely.

"Yes, you may. But Bernadette gets to blow it out tomorrow," Mama said.

"Enough about the candles!" Daddy put his knife and fork down on his plate. "We need more than candles for Advent. We need songs! So, let's sing an Advent song. 'O Come, O Come, Emmanuel,' is my favorite. Emmanuel is another name for Jesus, so that song asks Jesus to come," Daddy said. He looked at each of us. "When will He come?"

"Christmas!" Victor and I shouted together.

Mama and Daddy started singing, "O Come, O Come, Emmanuel."

"Hey," I said. "We're learning that one at school, too."

Daddy and Mama sang it the whole way through. Then Victor and I tried to join in. I knew most of the words. Victor got some of them. Matthew actually tried to sing, too. He doesn't really know too many words because he's so little.

But he likes to say "O-o-o-o-o-o-o" in a kind of singing voice when everybody else is singing. He's pretty funny when he does it.

"That's pretty good," Daddy said. His face got an excited look. "Let's try it in Latin now."

"Let's eat dinner now," Mama suggested. "I'm tired and hungry." She smiled a thin smile at Daddy and began dishing out the chicken casserole onto everyone's plates. "Maybe you can try it in Latin after we eat?"

Mama's getting ready to have another baby. I think that baby is taking up a lot of her food, because she's hungry a lot.

"No carrots for—PLEASE no carrots for me," Victor said as Mama dished up his dinner. She looked at him and scraped two pieces of carrot off his plate and back into the casserole. He still had four pieces of carrot on his plate. He made a grumpy face, but he didn't complain. He just scooted them way over to the edge with his fork.

"Mama, do you know if that baby is a boy or a girl?" I asked.

"No, Bernadette, I don't. Sometimes the doctors can find out, but we'll just wait until it's born to see."

"That is difficult," I said. "Because how will I know what to give it for Christmas if I don't know if it's a boy or a girl? I would like it to be a sister. Because I could really use a sister." I made a face at Matthew, who had apparently just figured out how to spill out his sippy cup. He was happily pouring milk into his casserole and mushing it up. I watched him smear a handful of milky casserole noodles into his hair. "I mean, look at Matthew! Yuck-o! A baby sister wouldn't do that. Also, if it's a baby sister, she'll want a more interesting present. Like something involving a shiny ribbon or a sparkly jewel. Victor and Matthew, well, I don't know what to give them." I looked at

Matthew's mess again. "Maybe something involving dirt?"

"I don't know, Bernadette," Mama said after she finished chewing the bite that was already in her mouth. "I think you were pretty messy before you were two." She glanced at Matthew again. "Well, maybe not quite as messy as Matthew!"

He squealed in delight at the attention and lobbed a handful of casserole noodles at the dog. That didn't go well with Daddy.

After the dog and noodle thing was handled, Mama continued. "I think either a tiny boy OR a tiny girl will be just delightful. The new baby will be so tiny on Christmas anyway, you don't need to get a present for him or her."

Lots of Latin

CHAPTER TWO

At school on Tuesday, we went straight to music class after our good morning prayer and announcements. We always have announcements, but a lot of the time nothing needs to be announced, so our principal, Sr. Teresa Jerome, just says, "May God bless your school day."

I love music class. Miss Faith, our music teacher, has the most beautiful hair. But even more

11

beautiful than her hair is her singing voice. When she sings a song with the class, I hate to join in and cover up her voice. All of our voices just sound loud. Her voice, though, can be loud or soft, and it always floats high up into the farthest top corner of the music room.

Miss Faith clapped her hands to get our attention. "Class!" she called merrily. "Class, we have a lot to cover today. I'm sure that Miss D has been teaching you all about Advent and helping you prepare for Christmas. I'm sure that at home you are helping your parents get decorations ready, that you're buying and making presents for your families, and shopping for all the special ingredients to bake great-grandma's ginger cranberry spice bread."

"Whose great-grandma has a ginger cranberry spice bread?" Maggie whispered to me so loudly it only barely counted as a whisper. She giggled, too. Maggie is my best friend, and she is always giggling about something.

Miss Faith clapped for attention again. "Here in music class, we must use the Advent season to learn Christmas music so that we will be properly ready to greet our little Lord Jesus with a happy—and well rehearsed—song. I'm sure you've learned some of these songs already in kindergarten or at home, but as first graders, I expect you to know all the words to several songs. Let's begin with 'O Come, O Come, Emmanuel,' our Advent carol."

Miss Faith put one palm outward toward the class so that we would know to remain silent. She began to sing, very softly. She was singing so softly that I leaned forward to hear her. I could just barely hear her delicate voice floating up to the ceiling. I leaned further forward and listened harder. I could practically hear Maggie and Florence listening hard on either side of me. They

were barely breathing as they strained to hear Miss Faith's voice floating toward us. I recognized the song as the one Miss D had helped us learn, that Daddy and Mama were teaching us to sing before dinner, and that we'd sung at Mass last Sunday. But with Miss Faith's voice, it did not march along, or hop from note to note, or trudge forward as it had those other times. It slowly grew and filled us with expectation and longing to hear the next note as each word whispered past my ear like a little angel of song. But the words seemed different. She did not ever get to "Rejoice! Rejoice!" Instead, she sang what sounded like "Cow Day! Cow Day! Emmanuel Now shay turn pro tay, Israel…" When her voice just faded out on the last syllable of the last word, the whole first grade was still leaning forward, straining to hear the whisper of that beautiful voice singing the heavenly song.

Miss Faith put her hand down. Linus' hand shot up and waved frantically at her.

"Yes, Linus?" she called on him.

"That is the same song Miss D taught us. But you don't have the right words. It's supposed to say 'Rejoice! Rejoice!' I don't know what you were saying. I couldn't understand it at all."

"So you were paying attention," Miss Faith said with a smile. "I sang different words, but not a different meaning. Those were the Latin words. This song was originally written in Latin and then translated into English, only rather recently, so that we could more easily understand it. However, I would like us to sing in Latin so that you can listen to the music. That floating, haunting melody should be ethereal—straight from heaven. Since you don't know what each Latin word means, you will better concentrate on the sound and shape of the note and the quality of your tone. I'll guide you through each syllable—the meaning is the same."

16

We struggled through those funny syllables for the rest of music class. Then I understood why Mama had preferred dinner to Daddy teaching us the Latin words. We never would have made it to the eating part if we had to wait for that! But wouldn't Daddy but surprised when I already knew them next time he tried.

At recess, Maggie could not stop exclaiming about Miss Faith's beautiful song. She promised me that she would learn every word of Latin so she could sing like that. But Maggie singing loudly against the wind as she stood under the slide on the playground was no comparison to Miss Faith. I could hardly recognize it as the same song. Actually, I'm not really too sure that Maggie got very many of the words right.

When she finally finished her performance, I asked, "Hey—did you notice what Miss Faith said about getting ready for Christmas? Are you doing that stuff?"

"You mean the ginger spice cranberry bread? Don't be crazy! She was just joking."

"No, not great-grandma's bread. I mean buying and making presents."

How was I going to buy presents for everyone? I had not counted my money in quite a while, but I was pretty sure there would not be enough to buy a present for Daddy and Mama and Victor and Matthew AND the new baby— whatever it was. And what about Grandma Anne? And Grandma and Grandpa Fleur? There was just no way!

"Maggie, there are just so many people in my family. I'll never find enough money to buy enough presents. How about you? Who are you buying presents for?"

Maggie was the youngest in her family. She had lots of older brothers and sisters. She was my best friend, and I didn't even know how many brothers and sisters she had. Her oldest sister was already married! Maggie was her flower girl last summer and told me all about the wedding and how beautiful her sister was and how handsome the groom Charles was.

"Charles is your brother-in-law now. Do you have to give him a present?"

"No. We do an exchange. That means we all pick one name out of a hat and get a present for that person. So we all get a real nice present, but we don't have to spend a gazillion dollars. Then all us kids usually make something extra nice for Mom and Dad. Like last year, Tom helped us make a new bench for the kitchen table. Mom loved it! Tom let me help stain it, too. Stain is like paint, but wood color. It was really fun."

Well, I thought, I don't have a brother who can help me build something, but maybe I could make some really nice presents? But what?

"And what about the broken smiles kids?" Maggie asked. "Are you going to give them a Christmas present?"

"I completely forgot. I don't know." The broken smiles kids were kids who were born with gaps in their lips. Miss D had a name for it—left lip and palette or something—and she showed us pictures of them. Our class was trying to collect enough money so that one of those kids could get the operation to fix her smile. It cost a lot, but we were excited and were pretty sure that if every kid in our class brought five dollars, we would have enough. That would be such a good thing to do. But how could I have a Christmas present to give to everybody? There were just so many people.

A Piecrust Party?

CHAPTER THREE

"Hi, Mama," I said as I wandered into the kitchen. "What's for dinner?"

"Chinese stir-fry," she answered without turning around from the broccoli she was chopping.

"With egg drop soup? May I do the egg drop part?" I love egg drop soup. Almost better than

21

eating its salty goodness is stirring in the eggs and watching them feather out into delicate strings in the hot soup. I could almost feel the scent of the gingery broth finding its way to my nose and making me hungry, hungry, hungry.

"If you do the egg drop soup, we will definitely have some." Mama turned around and smiled at me. "Can you find the recipe?" She pointed to the little box shaped like a house where the recipes lived. I started shuffling through them looking for "Egg Drop."

"Mama," I said, "Miss D announced Christmas party items today. That means the item each kid is supposed to bring to the Christmas party. I got piecrust. Is that super boring, or what?"

"I hope you have to bring it in before the party. I wouldn't want the entire first grade munching on balls of raw piecrust."

"Yeah. We bring it in a few days before and turn it into pumpkin pies. Andrew gets to bring pumpkin in a can. Maggie gets to bring milk in a can. Milk in a can—that's pretty fun! I have a note about it in my backpack. I think we bring it in next week."

"Please make sure to give me the note so I know when to send the piecrust to school with you."

"OK," I agreed. "I'll find it later. Here's the egg drop soup recipe." I started reading the recipe. It was one printed out from the computer, which was good. Mama has lots of other ones that are written out by hand in cursive. But I can't read cursive yet.

6 c. chicken broth, it began.

"What's a 'c'?" I asked Mama.

"Hmm? What?" she asked me back. She was puzzled.

"A 'c,'" I repeated. "The recipe says 'six c. chicken broth'."

Mama looked like she understood, and she nodded. "That means cups, six cups. But we don't have chicken broth. You can use six cups of water and add chicken bouillon."

She opened a cupboard and got out a huge measuring cup. I started measuring water into a pot. Mama turned on the flame under the burner for me. I'm not allowed to do that by myself yet. But that is fine with me because I can never tell exactly when the clicking sound will pop and blue flame will pour out of the burner. It startles me every time.

Then Mama helped me find the soy sauce and ginger and measure them into the newly made chicken broth. I stirred slowly, waiting for the broth to start boiling.

"Mama," I began, "what do you want for Christmas?"

Mama stopped chopping the long green onions for a moment and smiled. "Thank you for asking, Bernadette. I'm not sure." She paused and then said, "I think I'd just like to have this baby!" She looked down at that big tummy.

I looked at her big tummy, too, and scrunched up my mouth. "I don't think I can give you that."

Mama laughed. "I suppose not! Something you could give me that I would like…" She looked around the kitchen. "I could use a new rubber spatula. Or some new pot holders."

"Is piecrust hard to make?"

"Oh no. It's pretty easy. We'll be able to make it without any trouble. It only has a few ingredients. Look—your broth is boiling. Are your eggs ready to drop in?"

I held up the small measuring cup with the beaten eggs to show that it was ready. "You pour, Mama. I'll stir."

Mama slowly poured the eggs while I swirled them into the boiling hot broth with the wooden spoon. The bright yellow liquid turned into delicate strings of cooked, white egg as it spun around in the dark, salty broth. I kept swirling even after all the eggs were in, just watching and smelling the delicious soup.

Spatulas, pot holders, piecrust. What everyday, dull objects. None of them were unexpected, or beautiful, or spicy like egg drop soup. If any of those things were soup, they would be cream of boredom. Well, at least I did better than the poor kid who was stuck bringing in the paper napkins.

Secret Presents

CHAPTER FOUR

On Saturday morning after breakfast, Daddy popped into my room. I was working on drawing penguins. I thought some penguin pictures would make nice decorations for my walls. But I couldn't get them quite right. They just looked like lumpy black and white birds standing around.

"Bernadette, have you been Christmas shopping yet?" Daddy sat down on the edge of my bed.

"No, but I counted my money. I don't think I have enough dollars to buy Christmas presents for everyone, plus give some to the kids with the broken smiles. Plus, who knows what to give Matthew anyway? He's too destructive. Plus, Victor only wants presents that involve real lasers. Where do you even get real lasers? Especially if you need the kind that won't permanently damage anyone. Plus, that baby is not getting born, so who even knows what to give it when it doesn't even have a name! Plus, Mama—"

"Slow down!" Daddy grabbed my bed with both his hands like he was about to fall off. "Slow way down. Now, let's talk about these difficulties one at a time." He picked up a penguin I was drawing. "What's this?" He turned it different ways like he couldn't even figure out which side was the top. "A very short Indian with no hands?"

"Daddy!" I grabbed the picture away from him. "It's a penguin," I sighed, "but I can't quite make it look right."

"Hmmm. Maybe you just need a picture of a penguin to look at. Now, Christmas presents. We'll solve the penguin problem later. Start with lasers—that sounds like a fascinating problem. Tell me everything."

I told Daddy everything. And one by one, he thought of solutions to all the Christmas present problems until only one remained. Lasers. Broken smiles. Destructive Matthew. Pot holders. Baby. Even Daddy did not have the perfect solution for that hidden baby yet.

"But we'll keep thinking about it," Daddy promised. "Now, grab your $8.46 and let's go shopping!"

When we got home from shopping, I ran to my room before Mama could see what I had in my shopping bag. I closed my bedroom door—gently, because I'm pretty good about not slamming these days—and looked at the treasures. I tore open the thin plastic bag of the package of cloth loops. I had loops of every color! I took out my bright red, square loom and began stretching loops across the pegs. Yellow. Red. Green. Black. Purple. It was starting to look beautiful. This would make a wonderful, every-colored pot holder. Mama would be so happy with it! I owned so many loops, I could even make a pot holder for each grandma. Then, if I had enough time, I could make a second one for Mama. I wondered if Daddy would like a pot holder, too. He doesn't really cook too much. He mainly cooks coffee, which doesn't require pot holders.

Just as I was thinking about Daddy and what he might like for Christmas, I saw his head peeking through my doorway. "Daddy!" I cried, "Look!" I held up my loom with the beginning of my many-colored pot holder stretching across it. "Won't it be perfect? Do you like pot holders, too?"

"I do…" he said slowly, like he was trying to think of a pot holder that had been a really good friend to him but was not able to. "But I think I like lasers better." He winked at me. "And, I found this picture of a penguin for you," he said and handed me a happy, black and white penguin that he'd torn out of one of my old coloring books. "I think it's the legs that were giving you trouble." He pointed to the picture. "It appears that penguins do not have legs."

Mary Christmas

CHAPTER FIVE

On Tuesday, I looked around after school but saw no minivan waiting for me. I opened my backpack to hunt out my mittens. It was too cold to wait around with bare fingers. Then I heard a friendly honk from the line of cars waiting to pick up kids. Once, Daddy explained to me the difference between a friendly honk and an angry honk. We were waiting at a red light. When it turned green, the car in front of us kept waiting. So Daddy gave that driver a friendly honk. There were no traffic lights here, though. So I looked around for the friendly honker in the St. Cletus parking lot. Daddy's car was there!

"Daddy!" I shouted as I hopped in. "Where is everybody? Is Mama getting that baby born?"

"No, I don't think so. Victor and Matthew were with Grandma and Grandpa Fleur while Mama had a doctor appointment. She called me to ask me to come get you because the appointment was taking longer than she thought it would. She'll pick you up from my office when she's finished."

By the time Daddy was finished telling me all that, we were already halfway to his office. It's not too far from St. Cletus. You can actually walk there, but then it does seem far. If the weather does not require you to wear mittens, though, it is a nice walk.

"Do you want a hot chocolate or a soda?" Daddy asked as we walked past the coffee shop between the parking lot and his office. Mama makes hot chocolate at home for us sometimes, but I hardly ever get to have soda. Then I thought of the warmth of hot chocolate coming through its paper cup, through my mittens, right to my fingers. That made for a delicious thought. Also, at the coffee shop, they put whipped cream and swirls of chocolate syrup on top. Mama doesn't do that at home.

"Hot chocolate, please," I said.

At Daddy's office, he set me up at the meeting table in the middle of the large room. He gave me a container of glue, scissors, and a piece of cardboard. He walked across the room to his printer and picked up a picture. When he brought it to me, I saw that the picture showed Han Solo and

Princess Lea shooting laser guns around a corner. The bad guys were not in the picture.

"Here," he said. "This can be your present for Victor and Matthew. First you glue the picture on the cardboard. Then you cut it apart into puzzle pieces. Voilà, a puzzle! Victor puts it together: he has a present with lasers. Matthew takes it apart again: he has some destruction."

"Perfect!" I agreed with a smile. Daddy and I both got to work.

*   *   *

After Mama picked me up and we were home with the boys, she pulled a biggish, yellowish envelope out of her giant purse.

"Kids, look at this," she called. Victor and I crowded in to see what she had. Matthew looked over. He was sitting in the middle of the living

room pounding wooden pegs into a tiny wooden bench with a wooden hammer.

Destruction... I thought. *I guess he doesn't waste any time thinking about what he's going to do next.*

From out of the envelope, Mama pulled a strip of black and white pictures.

"It's Baby," she said, holding up the strip for us to see.

The first two did not look like much besides fuzzy grayness. Baby could have easily been mistaken for the distant galaxy that appears in the *Science for Young People* book on Miss D's quiet reading shelf. I've been choosing that one a lot lately. The next picture of Baby looked rather more like one of the comets in *Science for Young People.* But the third picture was different. It showed a baby's face. The baby was sleeping, with its tiny, skinny hands curled up under its chin.

Victor looked at Mama's big huge tummy and then back at the picture. "For real?"

Mama smiled and nodded, "Isn't it amazing to see? Doesn't Baby look just like Matthew did when he was tiny?"

"Does that mean it's a boy?" I asked.

"Well, you can't tell from the face," Mama said. "I didn't see if Baby's a boy or a girl. We'll just have to wait."

"Well, does it have a name yet?" I asked. "If you can see its face so perfectly, we should have something to call it."

"I think we'll wait until Baby is born for a permanent name. Especially since we don't know if we should pick a boy name or a girl name. But we could use a name until then. A temporary name. What name would you pick?"

"Caterpillar Tractor!" Victor yelled immediately. Had he already been thinking about a name for Baby? Or does he just shout words without thinking? It's hard to tell a lot of the time.

Mama laughed. "You may use that, Victor," she said. "But I just don't think I can call my baby Caterpillar."

"I know!" I shouted, "Mary Christmas! Spelled M-A-R-Y."

"At least until birth, Mary Christmas it is!" Mama agreed.

"You Ruined Christmas!"

CHAPTER SIX

The Advent wreath already had three
candles burning while we ate dinner that night.
Two purple ones and a pink one flickered in the
middle of the table. The pink one still stood tall
and straight. The purple one next to it burned
happily with lots of nice purple drips making trails
down both of its sides. The first purple candle had

already twinkled through a lot of dinners, and it was shrinking quickly.

"Daddy," I began. "Do you think that littlest candle will last all the way until Christmas?"

Daddy tilted his head to one side and looked at the candle. Then he tilted his head the other way.

"Let's see," he said. He licked his finger and held it in the air. "No wind." He checked his watch. "It's 6:48 p.m. Grace, are there any time changes between now and Christmas? Daylight savings or anything?"

Grace is Mama's name. She smiled and said no.

"Any leap days?"

"No." Mama answered again.

"Are these candles made of beeswax or paraffin? Or maybe tallow?"

"Daddy! Don't be so silly!" I said. Mama giggled. I gave her my best "I'm serious, young

43

lady" look. I don't think I look quite as serious as she does when she gives me that look, because she just winked at me and took another bite of her tomato salad.

"I just asked a simple question. Do you think the candle will get too short to burn any more before we get to Christmas?"

Mama laughed. "Today is Tuesday. Next Wednesday is Christmas Day. That's nine dinners. So, the boys and I won't light it during lunchtime anymore. And we might have to blow it out before dinner is quite ended. Then we'll be able to make it last all the way until Christmas."

"I concur," Daddy announced in his serious voice.

"What's 'concur'?" asked Victor.

"It means 'agree.' I agree."

"I concur!" echoed Victor in his best serious voice, which is not bad.

I sized up the candles again. Even with all of Mama's special measures, I was not convinced that the little candle would ever celebrate Christmas with us. "I'm not sure that I concur," I said.

Victor looked at me looking at the candles. He looked at Mama. He looked at Daddy. Before I realized what he was thinking, he blew hard and the flame on the littlest candle went out.

"Victor!" I objected. "Tonight's my turn! You knew that. You did it yesterday. Mama! You can't let him do that. You have to—"

Victor took a big breath and huffed and puffed, and the other two candles went out.

"Daddy!" I cried, "You can't let him do that! It's my turn! He did it on purpose!"

"Bernadette," said Mama, "please stop whining and crying."

"But Mama," I objected, "it's just not fair! How can you let him get away with that?"

"Bernadette," Mama repeated, "I can't talk to you about it if you keep whining like that. I try to keep track of whose—"

"It was MY TURN!" I shouted. "You need to light them again so I can blow them out!"

"Mama said we needed to blow them out before dinner was over. I just wanted to make sure the candles last until Christmas," Victor said, trying to look helpful and innocent. He did not look helpful and innocent to me. He look sneaky and greedy.

"STOP!" called Mama. "That is more than enough. Bernadette," she looked right at me as she said my name. "Bernadette, you know better than to cry like a baby about a silly thing like blowing out the candles. And you certainly know better than to tell me what I need to do about it. Victor," she turned to look at Mr. Helpful, "you knew it was not your turn. And if you forgot you certainly knew it after you blew out the first candle. But I

47

will not light the candles again. That's enough of this nonsense for tonight. I'm tired. And I'm hungry. Everyone please finish your dinner so we can all go to bed."

I stared down into my plate and used my fork to stab at a zucchini. Why were we eating zucchini in December? Isn't zucchini a summer squash? I pushed the zucchini through a puddle of chicken gravy and kept pushing it around. It made a little gravy trail on my plate. Tired and hungry. How boring to be tired and hungry so much.

I was embarrassed to have shouted and cried like a little baby. I did not want to look at Mama or Daddy. I peered at Victor. He was not embarrassed to have stolen my turn to blow the candles out. He was happily eating chicken and hiding his zucchini under his boiled potatoes. I peered at Daddy. He took a sip of his water. He did not have any zucchini on his plate. He doesn't like it. Mama doesn't make Daddy eat vegetables he does not like. Everyone else has to at least taste the vegetables.

"I'm sorry, Mama," I said very quietly. "I'll try not to argue and complain like that."

"Thank you, Bernadette. I appreciate that very much." Mama smiled a tired smile at me.

After that, we all finished dinner without too much talking. Matthew made silly noises and said baby things to make us laugh. Victor said silly things to make Matthew laugh. Mama and Daddy smiled at the boys' silliness and gently reminded them to be quieter at the table when they got too silly. I just ate my dinner. I did not want to play silly little brother nonsense. I was too tired of brothers.

After I was excused from the table, I cleared my dishes and went to get into my pajamas. I saw a red loop on the floor in the hallway just outside my door. I entered my room. I saw red, yellow, purple, green, and black loops everywhere! Loops of every color lay scattered about in a horrible ruin. On my bed sat the little red loom. Two hours ago, that loom held a half-finished pot holder that was supposed to become Mama's Christmas present. Now, it was entirely empty. Next to it lay a tangled mess of partly woven pot holder. It looked like a chewed up old sock. I could never fix it.

"DADDY!" I wailed. "Has Matthew been in my room?" I collapsed on the floor with a thud and started to cry. I did not want to act like a baby. But this could not be fixed. That little force of destruction needed to be stopped. Daddy came in and saw what had happened. Matthew wandered in behind him and started playing with the loops that he'd scattered everywhere.

"STOP THAT! Stop that right now, you little destroyer!" I shouted through my crying.

"It's OK, Bernadette," said Daddy. He scooped Matthew up. He must have put him in his crib, because I just heard Matthew start to cry. That's what he does if he gets set in his crib without a bottle and a song.

Daddy returned. He scooped me up off the floor and sat us both down on the bed. He gingerly picked up the ruined pot holder.

"Oww! It burns us!" he joked, using the same thin whiny voice he uses for Gollum the monster when he reads the hobbit story out loud to Matthew and me. Matthew mostly doesn't listen until Daddy gets to the funny voices. He dropped the pot holder like a hot potato.

"Don't, Daddy!" I ordered, trying not to smile. "This is serious!"

Daddy could tell I was working hard to stay mad. That just made him try another joke. He pinched the tangled pot holder between his thumb and pointer finger, like he didn't want to touch it at all. "Vhat do ve have here?" he asked using a strange accent and looking at me with squinty eyes. "Eet appears to be ze remnant of ze ancient mummy's bandages. But where has ze mummy himself gone?" He looked around, pretending to be afraid that a mummy might show up, demanding the pot holder bandages.

I giggled in spite of myself. "Is that accent supposed to be a French voice or a vampire?"

Daddy dropped the pot holder with a fake frown. "It was a mad scientist. I thought it was pretty good!" He gestured toward the hallway and Matthew's room. Matthew continued to howl noisily. "Hear that?"

"How could I not?"

"Does it make you feel better?" Daddy asked.

I shook my head no.

"I didn't think so," Daddy said. "So I better go release him and have a talk with him pretty soon. I'm really sorry he ruined the pot holder you were working on. I'll help you untangle it if you'd like. You might have enough loops to just begin a new one. I will tell Matthew that he was wrong to destroy your project and make such a mess. He will understand that for about three minutes. Then, because he is not even two years old yet, he will forget again and look for something else to destroy. So my recommendation to you is to find a safe place for your pot holder, somewhere that Mr. Destructo cannot reach. At least we can be sure he'll love the present you made him." Daddy kissed the top of my head. "Better?"

"A little," I sighed.

"I love you, Punkin Pie!"

"I love you, too, Daddy."

Pumpkin Pudding

CHAPTER SEVEN

Friday would be the last day of school before Christmas. That meant that it would also have Mass for the whole school with an address afterwards from Sr. Teresa Jerome. She always likes to address the students on special occasions. Then, after all that, would be our class Christmas party. I could hardly wait for the Christmas party. Miss D knew every Christmas carol ever. She would lead us in singing them. And, because Miss D was so much fun, she would be sure to have some other, wonderful things planned to make the Christmas party extra fun. We'd just have to wait and see what they were.

I would have fun with all my friends at school. And, best of all, after the party, school would be over until the New Year! We would go home and do all the wonderful, last things before Christmas. Get our tree, decorate it, wrap presents, bake Christmas cookies. Mama would play Christmas music on the piano, and she would play more Christmas music on CDs while we all decorated and wrapped and baked.

But I almost ruined all of that.

Thursday, I got to school right on time. Usually, I rush in just a minute after the tardy bell.

Before I had even stuffed my mittens into by backpack, Maggie poked me excitedly.

"Aren't you so excited?" she asked.

"About what?" Maggie was almost always excited about something. Sometimes I had a hard time keeping track of all her excitement.

"It's almost Christmas!" she squealed. "Today's the last day for getting ready at school!"

"Well that's not so special," I said. "The party isn't until tomorrow."

"But today we're getting ready!" Maggie was still squealing with excitement. "Today we're making pie!" She held up both her hands. "Look what I've got. *Canned milk!* Isn't that *funny*!"

All my morning happiness at being on time vanished. My face turned into a picture of first grade sadness.

"Maggie!" I wailed. "I forgot the piecrust!"

All in a flash, I realized what had happened. I never gave Mama the note. I told her we were having a party, but not when to bring my item. The note must have said for ingredient people to bring their items today. The people with items like cider or paper napkins would bring their items tomorrow. I told Mama I'd give it to her, but I never remembered to do it. I checked in my backpack. I didn't see any note. But I was sure that I had never taken it out.

"Maggie! What'll we do? Not even Miss D can make pies without piecrust."

"Maybe your Mom hasn't driven out of the parking lot yet," Maggie suggested. "Go check. If you find her, she could bring the crust in time. Otherwise, we'll be having pumpkin pudding for our Christmas party."

I peeked at Miss D. She wasn't starting class yet. So I dashed out to the parking lot. I saw a few kids being dropped off, but that was all. No navy blue minivan. I was doomed now. Doomed. The whole first grade would make and eat pumpkin pudding. Even when we were grown up, the boys would still tease me. They'd send Christmas cards to my house that said,

"Christmas in first grade was great

Especially the pumpkin pudding we ate!"

I drooped while I dragged myself back to the classroom. Miss D was beginning the day now. The morning prayer and announcement had finished while I was in the hallway. I tried to slide into my seat without being noticed. No such luck.

"What's wrong, Bernadette?" asked Miss D. "And where were you? I know you were here before the bell rang."

I didn't want to tell Miss D about the crust. It would ruin her party. I was still trying hard to think up a way to fix it.

"She forgot the piecrust," Maggie blurted out. "She was checking if her Mom was still in the parking lot."

"She wasn't," I added glumly.

Miss D nodded sympathetically. She didn't even look worried that the first grade would be condemned to celebrate Christmas with pumpkin pudding.

"I see," she said. "If you'd like, you may call your mother from the office. We're not making the pie until after lunch. But we'll make do if she can't make a special trip back to school. I know she must be very busy and also very tired right now."

Everyone knew we were waiting for the baby.

"Thank you, Miss D," I said very quietly. I slipped out of my seat and headed for the office.

I dialed the number. Five rings. Click. Mama's voice: "Hi! You've reached the West's! Please leave a message." *Beep!*

I left a message. "Uh, Mama. I forgot to give you the note about the Christmas party. It's tomorrow. But I was supposed to bring piecrust

59

today. Because after lunch we're making the pies. Or maybe we'll be making pumpkin pudding instead. Because that's what it would be without any crust." I almost hung up, but then I remembered: "It's Bernadette." Then I hung up.

I drooped again on my way back. Miss D was talking about verbs. Most of the kids were trying to listen. Most of them were not really succeeding, though. Andrew and Simon were looking out the window, hoping it would start to snow.

All five kids in the row nearest the activity table were looking at the pie ingredients lined up there. Cans of pumpkin and milk, brown sugar, several delightful little jars of spices, and three lovely big, heavy ceramic pie plates. Those were white on the inside and painted on the outside. One was yellow, and two were red. Those must be Miss D's. They looked so much prettier than Mama's blackened metal ones. Had any of those kids noticed the missing ingredient? Or did they suppose the crust was in the refrigerator in the teachers' lounge, with the eggs?

For sure the eggs were there. No one was sneaking in droopily from a hopeless phone call requesting emergency egg delivery.

*   *   *

The morning dragged on. Miss D did some math—adding with carrying. We did a math worksheet. We went to the library. All I could think about was pumpkin pudding. Lunchtime arrived. No Mama. No piecrust. I resigned myself to a doomed future involving pumpkin pudding—making it, eating it, and never-ending memories of it. I quietly ate my meatloaf sandwich. Maggie and Veronica chattered away happily next to me. They tried to be extra nice because they knew how I felt about the piecrusts. But I just couldn't find anything to chatter about. So I ate quietly.

I took the last place in line back to the classroom after lunch. I did not look forward to beginning the exciting Christmas preparations. It seemed that no one else knew about the great impending disaster.

We all took our seats. All around me, the entire first grade chattered excitedly. James and Andrew were hotly discussing the number of eggs required for each pie.

Miss D sent James to the teachers' lounge to fetch the eggs he had brought. Then she called for silence and began giving instructions on how we would all work together for the pies and other preparations.

I turned to look at the ingredient table. My eyes were surprised to notice a big rolling pin with red handles. It looked just like Mama's. Next to it was a funny shaped plastic bag.

Just then I caught Miss D's voice saying, "…Mrs. West, Bernadette's mother, brought us some piecrusts during lunch. So that is where we'll begin. Right after hand washing."

Miss D did not know exactly how to handle the balls of piecrust. I think she'd been imagining a perfect circle of crust that unrolls out of a long skinny box from the grocery store. Not Mama. She would not make pies that did not involve a rolling pin. But I knew exactly what to do. I spread out the clean, smooth dish towel that Mama had brought. I sprinkled it with flour—Mama left that for us too. I rolled the rolling pin in the flour and patted it until it was white all over. Now the crust would not stick to the rolling pin or the cloth. I carefully patted one of the lumps of piecrust until it was shaped like a perfect ball.

My heart started to flutter nervously. I looked like an expert, but I'd never rolled out a perfectly round crust all by myself. I had watched Mama do it. I had helped her lots. But she was always the one to even up the shape into a lovely circle. Miss D stood just behind me, watching with great interest.

I gently set the ball of crust in the center of the floured cloth. I took a deep breath to build my courage. I made a fist and pounded that dough right in its center. Now it had the shape of a very fat circle. I turned my head and smiled at Miss D. She giggled a little and watched me pick up the rolling pin. I began to roll. Just a little bit in each direction.

"Maggie, Angie, and Veronica," Miss D called. "You come join Bernadette at the piecrust station." She turned to face me. "Bernadette," she continued, "would you show the other children how to get the crust ready? Try to let everyone have a turn to roll."

She looked back at the rest of the class as the three girls crowded in next to me to find out what to do. "Class," Miss D continued, "I'll divide you up into different stations for pie making. Then

we'll rotate. That way, each of you will get a chance to do each step." Her voice grew quieter, and she said to me, "Bernadette, do you mind staying here to run the crust station?"

I smiled and shook my head no. I did not mind. It would be wonderful to be the only kid in charge of a station.

I floured and patted and rolled with each kid in the first grade. The crusts weren't perfectly round at the end, but they fit into the pie plates. I showed the other kids how to fold the big crust, then fold it again, then oh-so-carefully lift it into the pie plate. Then we opened it up and pinched down all the edges. At the end, we had three nice piecrusts lining those pretty dishes. I even got to be one of the helpers to carry a dish with Miss D to the teachers' lounge. She poured the dark orange, spicy pumpkin liquid in and popped them into the oven one by one.

We sat making other Christmas decorations and singing carols until school ended for the day. And the delicious, warm smell of pumpkin pie floated into our classroom, promising a lovely treat for tomorrow.

Where's That Baby?

CHAPTER EIGHT

"Mama! How did you do it?" I called as I hopped into the minivan after school. I was thinking about the three perfect pumpkin pies cooling in the teachers' lounge.

"Do what?" Mama asked.

"The piecrust! I called you and left a message that I forgot it. Did you hear the message?"

"No, I didn't. You must have called while we were at the grocery store. But I was buying the ingredients for our own Christmas baking. That made me remember that you had said something about piecrust. So I checked the note when we got home, and—"

"But I never gave you the note. You asked me to, but I never did it."

Mama smiled at me. "I just got it out of your backpack one night after you were in bed. Anyway, I checked it and saw that ingredients were supposed to be at school today. I already had piecrusts mixed up for our own pies, so we hopped back into the car to take them to school. Miss D was the only one in the room when I dropped them off. I would have come to find you, but the boys

69

were waiting in the car. I'm glad it all worked out for you."

I smiled back at Mama. "Thank you, Mama. It turned out perfectly! I got to be a hero and teach everyone—even Miss D!—how to roll out piecrust and put it in the plate and pinch the edges. The pumpkin pies look perfectly perfect."

I turned and made a face at Matthew, who was buckled into his car seat. He squealed and tried to make a funny face back at me. I laughed at him.

"Oh!" Mama said, putting a hand on her huge tummy. She looked startled for just a moment. Then she looked regular again.

"That baby is just too big to fit in there any longer!" she laughed.

"Good!" shouted Victor from the backseat. "I'm ready to see it!"

"Me, too. Should we call Daddy and tell him to take you to the hospital?" I grabbed her phone

from its spot between the two front seats. I liked it when Mama asked me to dial her phone.

Mama laughed again. "No need to call Daddy right now. I'm on your side, but I don't think that Baby is."

*   *   *

After we were home, I went to count how much money I had left to buy Christmas presents. That Baby was still a problem. How could I buy a present if I still didn't know to buy a girl present or a boy present? The Baby present was the only one left. I had two pot holders finished—one for Mommy and one for Daddy. The puzzle for Victor and Matthew was finished. Mama had a nice shirt for Daddy that she said could be from Victor and me together. I was working on another pot holder for Grandma Fleur. That just left Baby. And the kids with broken smiles.

I finished counting and got $6.12. Not too bad, but not too much either. I was planning to give five dollars to the smile kids. If I did that, I would only have $1.12 left to buy Baby a present. That would not buy very much of a present. It might be enough to buy a satin ribbon, though. If Baby is a girl, she would like a satin ribbon. I would like a girl baby better anyway. I had enough brothers already. Presents involving lasers and destruction were OK, but it would be nice to have a sister who would like a pretty present.

I counted the money again. It came out to $6.21 this time. I counted it a third time. $6.21 again. I must have accidentally counted a dime as a penny that first time. That seemed a little better, but still not great.

Daddy found me in my room when he got home from work.

"What're you up to all by yourself here, Punkin Pie? You look too serious."

I looked up from the stacks of coins on my bed and smiled big at Daddy. I like it when he calls me Punkin Pie.

"Did Mama tell you about the *real* pumpkin pie? We made it at school today. I was the only one who knew how to roll out piecrust. It was just *wonderful!*"

"Then why so serious?"

"I'm counting my money to finish Christmas shopping. Our class is trying to have each kid bring five dollars to give to the broken smile kids. If I give away five dollars, then I'll only have $1.21 left to buy Baby a present. That might be enough to buy a satin ribbon. But what if it's a boy? I don't know what that would buy for a boy. Boys don't want anything good anyway. But we still don't even know if it's a girl or a boy!"

"I see the problem." Daddy scratched my head thoughtfully. He collapsed himself onto my bed. Two dollar bills, nine quarters, twelve dimes, four nickels, and fifty-six pennies went tumbling everywhere.

"Daddy! I spent a long time organizing that!"

"Oh, money's not the most important part of this question, Bernadette. I need a comfortable place to think." He closed his eyes and pretended to sleep.

Fifteen seconds later, he popped his eyes open and sat up. "Eureka! I've got it!"

"Got what?" I was starting to scrape the change together to put back into my piggy bank.

"I've got your solution. Go ahead and give five dollars to the poor waifs with the broken smiles. A smile really goes a long way. They'll use that gift every day for the rest of their lives. Then, you have $1.21 left, still. Right?"

"Right."

"Well, even if Baby gets born tonight, he or she will be too small to notice what you give for a

Christmas present. And he or she won't really need anything and won't even really appreciate anything. Right?"

"Right again, but—"

"Don't interrupt!" He closed his eyes as if he were shutting me out of his brilliant thoughts. "I have not yet finished."

I stopped talking and made big eyes at Daddy. He could be so silly sometimes.

"OK," he continued, "Baby doesn't need anything, BUT Baby is a part of the family, so I understand why you want to give him or her something—even if it's a him. So, where are the tiny clothes you wore when you were a new baby? Let's give Baby those."

Daddy started opening up my drawers and closet, as if he would find them tucked away right there. As if I had worn them just last week, and they had been neatly put away with the rest of the laundry.

"Daddy, didn't I wear tiny girl clothes, though? What if Baby is a boy?"

"Ahh!" Daddy exclaimed. "Some things you wore were tiny girl clothes. But we didn't know you were a girl until we got a good look at you—after you were born. So we had these other clothes. They had no pink. They had no blue. They were just green and yellow and orange and colors like that. You just looked kind of like a colorful frog until some grandparents and other relatives felt sorry for you and gave you some tiny pink dresses and things. Those colorful frog clothes are what Baby needs."

I smiled. Daddy had done it again. It was a great solution. I was a little worried that maybe those clothes weren't really mine anymore, since Victor and Matthew had probably worn them when they were tiny. But Daddy pointed out that I had never told anyone I'd like to give them to my brothers. Mama just started letting Victor wear them. That meant Victor and Matthew had just been borrowing. They were still mine to give away. Mama would know where they were. Daddy said that after Mama told him the location, he would even help me pick out the best ones and wash them. That was a nice touch, I thought. Then they would not smell like Matthew.

Daddy helped me count up the change he had knocked over. We put five dollars into an envelope for me to take to school the next day. I drew a picture of a kid with a perfect smile on the front of the envelope.

Stirring up Cookies

CHAPTER NINE

At last! It was Christmas Eve. At breakfast, we lit all four candles, just because it was so exciting. The first candle hardly had anything left of itself, so we didn't leave them lit very long. Victor blew out two, and then I blew out two. It wasn't hard to share the blowing out when there were four candles lit.

After breakfast, Mama got out the wrapping paper and tape and scissors. Victor and I worked on wrapping presents—all by ourselves. Mama kept Matthew in the kitchen while she cleaned up from breakfast and got everything ready to make Christmas cookies.

Victor didn't really have any Christmas presents of his own to wrap. He just had presents that Mama had saved up in her closet. She let him pick out of those so he'd have presents to give Daddy and Matthew and me. I guess that's what I did when I was only four, too.

We carried our packages out to the living room and put them under the tree. Mama was not yet ready to made cookies. So we just sat under the tree for a long time. I flipped the lights on and off. Somehow, Victor figured out how to make them go to flashing. So we watched them flash for a while. Then we turned them back on solid.

Mama still was not ready for cookies. So we rearranged the packages under the tree. There were the ones that Victor and I had just wrapped. There were tiny packages for everyone from Uncle Max and Aunt Evelyn in Michigan. There were soft packages for everyone from Aunt Melissa and Uncle Doug, also in Michigan. They always gave us new shirts. Victor was too small to remember that, so I did not tell him. I figured I wouldn't ruin the surprise. There were interesting packages from Grandma Anne. There were no packages from Grandma and Grandpa Fleur because they lived nearby. They didn't need to mail theirs.

Mama came in. "Matthew is asleep," she said softly. Then she smiled. "Let's make some cookies."

Mama got out three recipes. "Here we go. Gingerbread men, spritz cookies, and honey spice with lemon glaze. We can make two kinds. Which shall we choose?"

"What's spritz cookies?" asked Victor. I was glad he asked, because I didn't know either.

"I'm not sure if we made those last year," Mama said. "It's a kind of little butter cookie that has different shapes. To get the shapes, you squeeze the batter through a little cookie machine. You load the batter in, give it a little twist, and out comes the cookie. I think my cookie press machine can make wreaths, Christmas trees, stars, and some other shapes like triangles and rectangles."

"How do they taste?" I asked.

"Mainly, they just taste like butter and sugar," Mama replied.

"Let's do those!" said Victor, "I want to try the cookie machine."

"Me too!" I agreed.

"Great!" said Mama.

Mama already had butter softening up on the counter since all Christmas cookies need butter. Victor unwrapped the butter and dumped it in the

mixing bowl. I poured in the sugar. Mama flipped on the mixer and whirred those two ingredients together. She added a little spoonful of vanilla. She turned the mixer off.

"May I taste?" My finger was already reaching out to the bowl, almost touching the butter and sugar.

"Did you two wash hands?" Mama answered.

Victor and I ran to wash our hands—with soap—in the bathroom. We ran back. Mama let us each have a tiny lick of the deliciousness of butter and sugar whipped up together with a bit of vanilla. Spritz cookies were going to be delicious. I got to crack the egg in. Then Mama mixed again. Victor sifted in some flour with a pinch of salt. Mama mixed. I sifted in some more of the flour and salt. Mama mixed. Victor finished the sifting. Mama finished the mixing.

"Time for the cookie machine!" Mama announced. She scooped the dough into a big tube and screwed the end on. She showed us how to give the handle a little twist, and out came the dough in a fancy cookie shape. The first three cookies Mama twisted out didn't look like anything. The third one was a perfect little circle of a wreath.

"The dough is in the right spot now," said Mama, scooping the first, funnily shaped cookies back into the mixing bowl. "Now you give it a try, Bernadette."

She handed me the cookie press, and I carefully twisted the handle. My first one came out like a huge blob. My second one came out too tiny. My third one looked pretty good. I did a whole row of darling little wreaths.

"Now it's your turn, Victor." Mama said. "Do you want to do wreaths, or change the picture?"

Victor chose to change the design. After a few tries, he had some nice looking tiny Christmas tree shapes. Mama did another row, then she popped the cookie sheet in the oven. We filled up four sheets with darling little spritz shapes before we used up all the dough. We had three layers of cookie racks filled with tiny cookies, making the entire house smell absolutely delicious.

"Now gingerbread men!" cried Victor. Mama sat down on a chair at the kitchen table. She took a long look at Victor. She took a short look at the clock on the microwave. She took a long look down the hall at the door to Matthew's bedroom.

"Well bless Matthew's little heart for taking such a good nap," she said softly. "But I'm afraid I'm just too wiped out to make any more cookies today. I'm going to have to cancel the gingerbread men. Can you two play quietly so I can lie down while Matthew is sleeping?"

We nodded yes. I was a little sad about the gingerbread men. I'd been imagining some nice decorations on mine. Frosting, sprinkles, gumdrops, yum.

"Daddy will be home in about an hour, and then it will be time to get ready for Mass," she said as she walked toward her bedroom. "Don't open any presents!" she added before she closed the door.

Victor and I sat looking at the tree, the lights, the presents, and the cookies. Then we practiced "Veni, Veni Emmanuel," for Mass. I was pretty sure Mass would start with one last round of the Advent carol in the dark. Then all the lights in the church would come on, the lights on the huge Christmas tree in the front of the church would come on, and Father would put the little statue of Baby Jesus in the manger—then it would be Christmas!

Christmas Morning!

CHAPTER TEN

I opened my eyes. I could tell by the brightness of the light shining between the cracks in my curtains that it was morning. I rolled over to close my eyes again. It felt pretty cold outside my flannel sheets and pile of snuggly blankets. *Wait...* I thought to myself ...*it's Christmas morning!*

I hopped out of bed and wiggled my feet into my pink bunny slippers. I put on my purple bathrobe. The sleeves were too short. It barely came down past my knees anymore. But it was still pretty warm. I listened at the door of my bedroom. I did not hear anyone else awake.

I went into Victor and Matthew's room. They were both still sleeping. Matthew was curled up in a ball, drooling. I pulled his blanket up over him. He squiggled a little, but did not open his eyes. I tiptoed over to Victor's bed. His foot was hanging out over the edge of his bed. I tickled it a little. He wiggled, kicked at me, and rolled over. But he did not wake up.

I sat down in the middle of the floor. I waited for a minute or two. The boys were still asleep. I tiptoed over to their window and lifted up the corner of the curtain to peek outside. There was snow! Not a lot, but just enough to make everything white and sparkly and beautiful under the sunny, bright blue sky. I gazed at the snow for a while and pressed my nose against the icy cold glass. Then I heard Victor's voice.

"What are you doing, Bernadette?"

I dropped the curtain and turned around, "It snowed in the night! And it's Christmas!" I helped Victor find his slippers and tie the rope of his bathrobe. Then we went down the hall to tell Mama and Daddy that it was Christmas. Quietly, we opened the door of their bedroom. The bed was made, and no one was sleeping in it. *Very strange,* I thought. We walked back down the hall. Matthew was awake now, so I pulled him out of his crib. He had sleepers on, so he did not need slippers. We all went downstairs.

The Christmas tree lights were on, sun shone in through the big living room windows, and there on the couch, lay Grandpa Fleur—snoozing. What

was he doing here? When we came into the living room, Grandpa sat up a little and rubbed his eyes.

"*Christus natus est!*" he said.

We all just looked at him suspiciously.

"Where are Mama and Daddy?" I asked. "And what are you talking about? You sound like a rooster."

"*Christus natus est!*" Grandpa repeated, making it sound even more like a rooster this time. "That's Latin. It means, 'Christ is born!' Merry Christmas! And you're right, that is what the rooster said on the first Christmas morning. All the animals could speak on that first Christmas morning—the only day in the history of man that they could speak. And wouldn't you know they spoke Latin?" He smiled as he checked his watch.

"Your Mom and Dad left for the hospital about two hours ago. It seems that the baby wasn't willing to miss Christmas. Grandma's in the kitchen making pancakes and kielbasa. Let's see if

92

it's ready, and I'll tell you what the rest of the animals said on Christmas morning."

The baby! Well how about that! A Christmas baby. Christmas wouldn't be the same without Mama and Daddy, but they'd come home tomorrow with our new baby!

We all sat down to Grandma's breakfast. Grandpa brought over mugs of hot chocolate for us. He even gave Matthew a breakable mug. Then he poured himself a coffee and sat down at the end of the table.

"*Christus natus est!*" He crowed for a third time, sounding quite like a rooster. "That's what the rooster called to the town of Bethlehem on that first Christmas morning so long ago, the very morning when Jesus was born."

"Is OUR baby born yet?" I asked.

"They said they'd call when the baby is born," Grandpa replied. "Now, do I have to do the rooster again? Or may I continue where I left off?"

93

He gave me the look. He has a look that is only from him. It's not really scary, like the look Daddy has when he's mad. It's not disappointed, like the look Mama has when I've done something wrong. It's just *serious*. It's a look I do not like getting.

"Sorry," I said quietly.

Grandpa continued. "Well, when the rooster broke the silence of the night with that great announcement, he opened the mouths of all the other animals, and they began to answer him. '*U-u-u-ubi? U-u-u-ubi?*'—that means 'Where? Where?'—called the cow."

Matthew laughed at the way Grandpa made himself sound like a cow when he said the words.

"Do you know who answered the cow's question?" Grandpa asked us.

We all shook our heads.

"The mama sheep answered with, '*Be-e-et-lem. Be-e-et-lem.*' That's the Latin for Bethlehem,

94

the name of the city where Jesus was born. And then her little lamb was so excited to hear the news, he stood up and baa-aa-ed out: '*E-a-a-a-mus! E-a-a-a-mus!*'"

We all laughed that time. Grandpa made such a funny, perfect little voice for the baby lamb.

"That means, 'Let's go! Let's go!' The other big animals heard the lamb and looked around, wondering what to do. But the little calf scrambled to her feet and said in her little mooing voice, '*Vo-o-o-lo! Vo-o-o-lo!*' That means, 'I will! I will!' So, all the animals spoke at once, and soon their noisy chatter woke up the people, who followed their animals to the stable in Bethlehem where they all knelt before the newborn baby Jesus."

I clapped for Grandpa's story, and Grandma and Victor clapped with me. Matthew just laughed and smeared syrup into his hair. Then the phone rang.

My eyes got big. "It's the baby!" I shouted. "Hurray for our Christmas baby!" Victor and Matthew joined me in shouting and hooting, and we filled up the room with our excited noisiness.

"Hush! Hush!" Grandma called at us as she hurried over to answer the phone. "I won't be able to hear the news."

Victor and I got quiet immediately. Matthew didn't, but I was pretty sure Grandma would be able to hear over the noise of just one kid with syrup in his hair. Grandpa and I watched as Grandma nodded and smiled and nodded again. "Well, that's just wonderful!" she gushed. "Give them both our love. Bye."

I must have looked ready to burst with trying not to shout and demand to know.

Grandma turned back toward the table. "It's a girl! Mama and Baby Natalie are both doing just fine. Your Daddy says we can head over for a visit after lunch, which leaves plenty of time to open some presents now."

A baby sister! Just what I wanted! And we'd get to see Mama and Daddy later on—and take them the presents I'd made them. And also meet our new baby SISTER! This was the perfect Christmas.

About the Author

Emily Ortega earned a Bachelor of Science in chemistry from Case Western Reserve University. After working for two years as a campus missionary with FOCUS, the Fellowship of Catholic University Students, Emily earned her Master's degree in Humanities from Stanford University. She currently resides with her husband and their seven children in Santa Fe, New Mexico. She's excited to bring a fictional Catholic family to life and offer young Catholic readers the possibility that their lives in a big, Catholic family aren't really that odd.

About the Illustrator

Meg Whalen was born in Michigan, but grew up in Florida near the ocean. She has always enjoyed drawing and had a comic strip when she was a girl, but it wasn't until much later that she decided to pursue a career in children's books. After converting to Catholicism, Meg moved to Colorado to study theology at the Augustine Institute and to train in illustration at Rocky Mountain College of Art & Design. She resides in Denver with her husband Danny.

CPSIA information can be obtained at www.ICGtesting.com
Printed in the USA
LVOW04s2149150415

434796LV00012B/132/P

9 781500 966966